NIGHTMARE

Titles in Teen Reads:

Copy Cat	**Fair Game**	**Mama Barkfingers**
TOMMY DONBAVAND	ALAN DURANT	CAVAN SCOTT
Dead Scared	**Jigsaw Lady**	**Pest Control**
TOMMY DONBAVAND	TONY LEE	CAVAN SCOTT
Just Bite	**Mister Scratch**	**The Hunted**
TOMMY DONBAVAND	TONY LEE	CAVAN SCOTT
Home	**Stalker**	**The Changeling**
TOMMY DONBAVAND	TONY LEE	CAVAN SCOTT
Kidnap	**Dawn of the Daves**	**Nightmare**
TOMMY DONBAVAND	TIM COLLINS	ANN EVANS
Ward 13	**Joke Shop**	**Sitting Target**
TOMMY DONBAVAND	TIM COLLINS	JOHN TOWNSEND
Deadly Mission	**The Locals**	**Snow White, Black Heart**
MARK WRIGHT	TIM COLLINS	JACQUELINE RAYNER
Ghost Bell	**Troll**	**The Wishing Doll**
MARK WRIGHT	TIM COLLINS	BEVERLY SANFORD
The Corridor	**Insectoids**	**Underworld**
MARK WRIGHT	ROGER HURN	SIMON CHESHIRE
Death Road	**Billy Button**	**World Without Words**
JON MAYHEW	CAVAN SCOTT	JONNY ZUCKER

Badger Publishing Limited, Oldmedow Road, Hardwick Industrial Estate, King's Lynn PE30 4JJ
Telephone: 01438 791037

www.badgerlearning.co.uk

NIGHTMARE

ANN EVANS

Nightmare ISBN 978-1-78147-972-8

Text © Ann Evans 2014
Complete work © Badger Publishing Limited 2014

All rights reserved. No part of this publication may be
reproduced, stored in any form or by any means mechanical,
electronic, recording or otherwise without the prior permission
of the publisher.

The right of Ann Evans to be identified as author of this Work has
been asserted by her in accordance with the Copyright, Designs and
Patents Act 1988.

Publisher: Susan Ross
Senior Editor: Danny Pearson
Publishing Assistant: Claire Morgan
Copyeditor: Cheryl Lanyon
Designer: Bigtop Design Ltd

8 10 9 7

CHAPTER 1

HASTY WORDS

Midnight – and Todd awoke in a sweat again. A cold sweat, making the sheets stick to his clammy skin, making his heart thump. Sleep was rare these nights, since…

He swung his legs out of bed and sat, head in hands. Of course he couldn't sleep. He couldn't sleep because he was riddled with guilt.

He hadn't meant to be so spiteful. When weirdo Elspeth from his class asked him out, he didn't mean to humiliate her – destroy her. Only all his mates were watching and he'd felt embarrassed.

So he'd looked down his nose like she was a bit of dirt on his shoe. He'd laughed – loudly – and then mocked her. His words ran through his mind…
Go out with you! Have you looked in the mirror lately?
And then came the crunch. The killer blow that sent tears flooding down her scarlet cheeks. The words that sent her scuttling away out of sight…
I'd have to be blind to date you!

She'd stayed off school for ages afterwards. Too humiliated to face anyone.

Now she was back but she hadn't spoken to him. She'd looked though. She hadn't stopped looking – from the corner of her eye. Sharp, mean, hateful glances. Like she wanted him dead.

Todd stared at his reflection in the mirror. His face was pale, gaunt. His eyes red and baggy. His appetite had deserted him since the nightmares started, so he'd lost weight. He looked a right mess.

His chances of dating Lexie were diminishing rapidly. Unless she fancied guys who looked like zombies. Somehow he didn't think she did. But that was how his sleepless nights were making him look – like a zombie.

It was the same nightmare night after night. A face looming up at him. A hideous, grey-white face. Just a face, no body. A head. A decapitated head, growing in vileness until it filled his mind. Its mouth was open in a silent scream. Eyes were black hollow sockets – soulless. It swayed there, in his dreams, like a lantern on a tree.

Every night he awoke sweating, heart slamming against his ribcage. It was a relief when morning came. Now another long day at school stretched before him.

"Hey, Todd!" Webby yelled as Todd shuffled into class. "You look knackered. Late night?"

"Yeah, went to a party," he lied. He could hardly say bad dreams had kept him awake all night. He'd be labelled a wuss!

Lexie – gorgeous Lexie – was at her desk. She glanced up, smiled shyly at him. Then she frowned. "You OK?" she murmured.

"Yeah, good thanks."

"You don't look it."

Webby jabbed him in the ribs and winked.

Despite feeling a wreck, Lexie's concern cheered Todd up. Until he spotted Elspeth's narrow eyes fixed on him. She didn't look away even though he'd caught her staring. She just squeezed her eyes even tighter until they were slits. Like a snake's. And probably as venomous.

At break time Lexie met him in the playground. His heart began to race – but in a good way. She was so pretty. She had the softest fair hair, the brightest green eyes. She was really smart too. Top in most subjects.

"Todd, I'm worried about you," she said, sitting beside him on a bench. "You look ill. Are you sick?"

He couldn't lie to Lexie. She'd see through him and wouldn't be impressed. And he really wanted her to like him. For weeks he'd been trying to pluck up the courage to ask her out. It would serve him right if she turned him down. Made a fool out of him. Like he'd done to Elspeth.

He glanced across the playground. Elspeth was standing there. Staring at him. Glaring at him. Weird, skinny Elspeth with her straight, mousy hair and cold eyes. He wished he'd turned her down gently, though.

"I'm not sleeping," he told Lexie.

"Why?" she asked.

He took a deep breath. "Nightmares. Well, the same recurring nightmare. It wakes me up. Then I can't get back to sleep. And if I do, it comes back. Every night. Every single night for weeks."

His voice had risen. He sounded desperate even to his own ears.

Lexie didn't laugh. She rested her hand on his and looked into his eyes. "That's awful. Have you seen a doctor?"

"No, only a severed head," he joked. He was glad he could still make jokes. He wasn't a complete zombie yet.

She looked horrified. "A what?"

"That's my nightmare. Same thing every time. A decapitated head with gaping holes where its eyes ought to be. It looms up at me like it's going to swallow me. It gets closer and closer till it's right here." He put his hand a centimetre from his face. "That's when I wake up sweating and shaking."

"You need to see someone," Lexie said anxiously. "A sleep therapist, or a… er… psychiatrist. Sorry!"

Todd lowered his head, guilt swamping him again. "Actually, Lexie, I think I know what's causing the nightmares."

"You do? What?"

He pulled a face. "Er... my guilty conscience."

She moved a little away from him. "Oh! What have you got to feel guilty about?"

Heat scorched his neck. "Er… Elspeth asked me out…"

She looked sad suddenly. "Oh! Did you go?"

"No, 'course not. Only the way I turned her down wasn't nice." He lowered his voice. "I made her look a fool. Made her cry."

"Oh poor Elspeth," Lexie said, horrified. "That girl has no friends. It must have taken so much courage to ask you out."

"Yeah, I know. I didn't mean to be so horrible. Only Webby and the others were watching, smirking, muttering stuff. So I just said all sorts of stupid things." Lexie was still looking horrified. She probably hated him. Panicking now he ranted on, "I shouldn't have. I'm not normally like that…"

To his amazement, she took his hand. "I know you're not like that. You're sweet – normally."

His mouth dropped open. "Am I?"

She smiled and the dimples deepened in her cheeks. "Of course you're sweet or I wouldn't like you, would I?"

Todd felt his insides turn to goo. His words tumbled over each other as they tried to get out of his mouth. "You… er… you like me? Really?"

She leaned towards him. Her scent made him dizzy. And then she kissed his cheek and his world turned upside-down.

If only Elspeth hadn't been standing watching, glowering at him, life would have been perfect. But those daggers in her eyes felt like they were being hurtled his way, each one thudding into his chest.

CHAPTER 2

SPECIAL POWERS

As Todd drifted off to sleep his thoughts were on Lexie. Her scent, her touch, her kiss. Her lovely face drifted into his mind. Closer and closer she came. Her lips parted in a smile as the heaviness of sleep closed over him.

But what was going on? Her mouth continued to widen. Her teeth glinted white... and then sharpened to points. Like little daggers. Two rows of jagged daggers set within a gaping black hole. And then dark red goo began to ooze out from between the pointed teeth. It trickled down her pale chin – blood. Her green eyes rolled upwards and fell backwards into black, hollow eye-sockets.

Todd's shriek echoed around his bedroom walls as he sat bolt upright. Sweating. Shaking. He lay awake the rest of the night.

Next morning, Webby and the others were hanging around the playground in no hurry to go into class. Webby grabbed him round the neck, grinning. "Look at you! Another late night? You sure know how to party!"

His mates crowded round, wanting to know what he'd been up to. He spotted Lexie in the background. But before he could say anything to anyone, Elspeth pushed her way through the crowd. She stood right in front of him, hands on hips.

A hubbub of whispers sprang up. Then fell silent as Elspeth spoke. "I believe you're having trouble sleeping at night?"

This was a new Elspeth. Sure of herself. Todd tried to find some witty reply but his mind went blank. The confident way she was looking at him was weirdly unnerving.

She shifted from one foot to the other, seeming bored. "I said you're having trouble sleeping, aren't you?"

"What makes you think that?" Todd asked, glancing at his mates. They'd take the mickey mercilessly if they knew the truth.

Elspeth's pale eyes speared his. They were unnaturally pale, silvery, not quite human. "I just know," she said. "I have certain powers."

Webby and the others burst out laughing. Todd expected her to burst into tears and run away. But she didn't. She didn't even flinch. More kids gathered round, curious to know what was going on.

"Tell me about your dreams," said Elspeth, her voice low, hypnotic. "Tell me about those nightmares that stop you from sleeping."

Todd wanted to break away. But it was like she was holding him spellbound. Lexie must have told her. No one else knew.

"Tell me," Elspeth urged. "I can help."

"Yeah! Go on. Tell her about your nasty old nightmares!" laughed Webby. The others joined in.

"OK!" Todd yelled, spotting Lexie in the crowd. He lowered his voice. "Every night I'll be dreaming, nice things sometimes, when it suddenly changes. A face appears. A horrible, white, severed head, dripping blood…"

All around him, Todd heard his mates making yeuk and sicky noises. He ignored them. Transfixed by Elspeth.

"And you wake up terrified. Poor Todd!" she murmured. "Shall I make the nightmares stop?"

Todd hadn't meant to laugh. It wasn't a real laugh anyway, more a snort of disbelief.

Elspeth raised her eyebrows. "You don't think I can?"

"No! How could you?" Todd asked in disbelief. Although he was positive it was because of her, sort of, that he was getting bad dreams.

"But I can," Elspeth promised, smiling at him now. "I can take away these frightening dreams. I can make you sleep peacefully at night again."

"How?"

Her pale eyes didn't blink. "It doesn't matter how. It matters that I can."

She unnerved him. Weird Elspeth gave him the creeps. He didn't like the way she was looking at him – through him. For a second it was like she was reading his mind. Somehow he managed a cocky smile. "Well go on then. Work your magic."

"It'll cost you."

He hadn't thought of her as a money-grabber. But now he grinned at his mates. As if he'd expected this all along. "Go on, how much?"

"Not much. Just a kiss," came her reply.

"A kiss!" Todd exclaimed as hoots and whistles exploded all around him.

Elspeth looked at him innocently. "Is that too much to ask?"

Todd scratched his head. "Just a kiss?"

"Yes. Just a kiss."

He took her arm. Steering her away from the crowd. In a whisper he said, "Not… er… not like the whole thing? Then you demand money for your services or something? Like someone's going to beat me up if I don't cough up?"

She didn't seem offended despite what he'd just said. "Kiss me here. In the playground. Now, in front of your friends. They can be witnesses. It's just a kiss."

Webby sauntered over, a Cheshire Cat smile on his face. "Go on, Todd. You don't get an offer like that every day. Anyway, what you got to lose?"

Todd hesitated. This was a trick. She was probably going to wind him up. Pretend to let him kiss her then kick him in the whatsits. Get her revenge for him humiliating her.

Well, if that's what it took to ease his guilty conscience, he'd do it. He didn't want to kiss Elspeth though. She was horrible and weird. He wanted to kiss Lexie. She was still there, in the crowd. But now she had her head down, staring at her feet.

Webby was getting impatient. He pushed in front of Todd, a stupid expression on his face. "Actually, sweetheart, I'm getting nightmares too…"

Elspeth flashed him a fierce look. "That could be arranged!"

Webby backed off.

Elspeth pointed a finger at Todd, like a witch casting a spell. "I can only stop Todd's nightmares." Then she looked him right in the eye. "Well Todd? Are you going to kiss me or not?"

CHAPTER 3

THE KISS

Todd rubbed his sweaty palms down his trouser legs. "A kiss? And the nightmares stop, yes?"

"That's what I said."

Behind him everyone was whooping and egging him on. He didn't want to look at Lexie. This was so wrong. But if it could put an end to his nightmares he had to do it.

"Get on with it!" someone yelled.

Todd took a deep breath. It was only a kiss. No big deal. He took a step towards her, expecting her knee to come up into his groin at any second. Her arms went around his neck drawing him closer. He got the sinking feeling that he wasn't going to get away with a quick peck on the cheek.

As Elspeth's lips touched his, a great cheer went up from his mates. She half closed her eyes. He kept his wide open and saw she was looking at him through slits. Now she looked even more venomous.

She was making a meal of it and he pulled back – or tried to. But it was difficult, her mouth was too eager, too demanding. She was sucking on his lips and sucking the breath from his lungs.

He tried to disentangle himself from her. She wasn't that big. She didn't look physically stronger than him. But he couldn't break free.

The cheering got louder.

Her face was over his. Her cheek pressed over his nostrils. Her lips clamped over his. Todd tried to gasp some air out of the corner of his mouth, but her mouth smothered even this last, tiny lifeline. He was suffocating.

Struggling, he tried to push her away. Instantly her arms slid down from around his neck to pin his arms to his sides. Panic flared inside him. She was ridiculously strong.

Struggling, writhing, he heard the cheering, the hooting, the whistling. Like it was the wildest thing they'd ever seen. A clammy blackness swept over him. Somewhere far away he thought he heard Lexie sob his name. Then blackness swamped him.

His lungs were empty, they felt like deflated balloons and the pain was agonising. Slowly the strength was slipping from his body. Now it was hard to keep standing. He tried to fall. At least if he collapsed people would realise she was trying to kill him. But she was holding him up, stopping him from crumpling to the floor.

Thoughts flashed through his brain. His mum, dad, gran, starting school, toys… years flicked through his head like a reel from a silent movie. He was dying. Elspeth had her revenge. She was killing him.

And then she released him.

His legs buckled and he drew in a breath that would surely empty the world of oxygen.

Webby slapped him enviously on the back. "You lucky so-and-so!"

Todd couldn't speak. He wanted to slap her. No, worse, he wanted to throttle her!

Elspeth stood there cool as a cucumber despite knowing she'd almost killed him. Despite seeing the look in his eyes that said he wanted to murder her.

She simply looked innocently at him and calmly said, "There! No more night time bad dreams."

And amid more whistles and hoots she walked, head held high, into class.

"Jeezuzz!" Webby whooped. "Well, who'd have thought mousy Elspeth was that hot! Todd, my man, you are one lucky, lucky babe magnet!"

In a way, Todd did feel lucky. Lucky to be alive.

As the crowd dispersed and went into school, Todd looked around for Lexie. She was nowhere to be seen. He caught up with her in class but she had her head in a book and didn't glance at him.

Elspeth sat eagerly at her desk, looking pleased with herself. Todd groaned and tried to concentrate on some work.

He dreaded going to bed that night. Positive the nightmares would be there, waiting for him. But amazingly, for the first time in weeks he slept well. His dreams were ordinary. Wonderfully ordinary. No nightmarish, decapitated head looming up at him. He didn't wake in a cold sweat in the middle of the night. It was the same the following night, and the next.

It had to be coincidence. Elspeth couldn't have banished his nightmares just by kissing him… or rather, practically suffocating him. Unless that was her trick, take him to the point of death and bring him back. Something must have clicked in his brain and done away with the nightmares.

All he had to do now was get Lexie to talk to him again and life would be good.

He spotted her walking along the street towards school. Breaking into a run he quickly caught up with her. She didn't look pleased to see him.

"Lexie, please, let me explain."

"Nothing to explain," she said coolly, quickening her pace.

"Lexie, please... she said she could stop the nightmares if I kissed her."

"And you believed her?" Lexie said sharply. "She fancies you. It was a trick. And you fell for it. Or maybe you wanted to kiss her. I must say she seemed very good at it."

"She was trying to suffocate me..."

"Spare me the details!"

"Lexie!" Todd begged, touching her arm. She shrugged him off. "Well if you hadn't told her about my nightmares it wouldn't have happened. I told you that in confidence you know."

She stopped abruptly. "I didn't tell her!"

Todd frowned. "Then how did she know?"

"You must have told her."

"I didn't!" he protested.

They stood staring at each other. Then Lexie asked softly. "How are the nightmares, anyway?"

"All gone!" Todd exclaimed, delighted. "I haven't had a nightmare in three nights now."

"Really?"

"Absolutely. I've been sleeping well," Todd said. Then, risking a light touch of his hand on hers, added, "Well, except for worrying about you. I never meant to hurt to you, Lexie."

She gazed at him for long seconds, her green eyes searching his face. Seeing if she could trust him. And then she smiled and her hand closed around his. They walked into class hand in hand.

He didn't give Elspeth a second thought. It was only when he glanced across the classroom that he saw her glaring at him. Eyes narrowed to slits of hatred. And he shuddered.

CHAPTER 4

THE BEAUTIFUL GAME

There was a football match after school. Lexie said she'd stay behind and watch. The opposition were from the Grammar School and it was always a close game. Webby wasn't in the team, he didn't believe in breaking a sweat. But he and some of the others stayed to support.

Todd ran out onto the pitch to their cheers. But his smile faded when he spotted Elspeth standing on the far side of the pitch. He deliberately ignored her as the game got under way. As goalkeeper, he had a tough time keeping the ball out of the net. Five minutes before the end, the score was nil–nil.

Suddenly their striker burst through, running like a demon, dodging the defenders, his eyes set on the goal. He took an almighty kick sending it hurtling directly at him.

Todd was ready, timing it, ready to leap into the air and punch it to safety. His eyes were fixed on the spinning ball... but it wasn't a ball. The thing hurtling through the air was a severed head, red eyes bulging, blood and sinews trailing behind it. Coming at him! Straight at him! There was only one thing to do.

He ducked!

As the opposition danced about hugging each other, Todd looked helplessly at them. What the hell was the matter with them? Didn't they see it was a severed head the striker had just kicked?

He glanced to where Lexie and his mates were. They were standing open-mouthed with disappointment. Looking behind him into the net, expecting to see a vile, decapitated head, he saw – a football.

No one believed his story when he tried to explain what he'd seen. Walking home later, Lexie suggested he made an appointment with a doctor.

He dragged himself home, feeling wretched. Nearing his house he stopped, his heart jumping into his throat. There was something dangling from the bracket where his mum's hanging basket normally hung. Something pale. A sickly, greyish-white thing.

He stumbled. His feet didn't want to take him any further.

He knew what it was. Deathly grey skin, hollow eye-sockets, blood dripping from its open, gaping mouth. He felt the scream building up inside him. It dangled there, swaying slightly in the breeze. A severed head instead of a pot full of geraniums. And as it swung, a mass of red tendrils, dripping blood, dropped from its severed neck and dangled there like ribbons.

Todd shrieked and turning, panic-stricken, slammed straight into a lamppost.

He came to with a dull ache in his forehead. Something white was hovering over him and he lashed out, frantically trying to push it away. Coming fully awake he saw it was just a nurse in a white uniform. They'd put five stitches into the gash.

Webby winced in sympathy two days later when Todd was well enough to go back to school. Lexie planted a little kiss on his forehead, which made him feel a lot better. He told them what he'd seen.

Webby stared at him. "Nah! You're dreaming, mate."

Todd wished more than anything that he had been dreaming.

He was walking home when it happened again. Walking past a telegraph pole, he happened to glance up and it was there. That same hideous, grey abomination dangling from the telegraph wire.

Stifling the scream that swept up from his chest, he broke into a run. When he looked back it had gone.

But it was waiting for him at home.

It was hiding in the bottom of his wardrobe amongst his shoes. Red-veined eyes rolled upwards to look at him and then rolled into the back of its head, leaving just the blank, deathly sockets.

It was dancing like a stringless puppet behind him when he looked in the bathroom mirror. And when he woke in the morning it was there, on the pillow next to him.

Next day, Webby looked him up and down. "You look a mess, mate."

Todd kept his eyes down. Tried not to look up at the ceiling where he could see it from the corner of his eye. Dangling from the light fitting. At this rate he would have to see a shrink. It was only Lexie's concern that kept him going.

"I have an idea," Lexie said, taking his hand and leading him behind the cycle sheds.

"Well, I like it so far," Todd said, pleased to know he could still smile.

Out of sight of everyone she took his face in both hands. "If Elspeth's kiss got rid of your nightmares, maybe a kiss from me will cure your hallucinations."

Todd slid his arms around her waist. "It's worth a try!"

She had to stretch up on tiptoe, and for a second all Todd's worries vanished. She smelled so nice and her skin was so soft. Through half-closed eyes he brought his face close to hers.

Red veined, bulbous eyes blinked up at him. Then fell backwards leaving just two bleak, empty holes. She smiled and blood oozed from between her teeth. With a scream Todd pushed her away, jumped back, flattened himself against the wall, breathing raggedly. A look of horror plastered all over his face.

Lexie's face, normal now, crumpled into utter misery. Tears filled her beautiful eyes. She turned and ran before they could fall.

"Lexie! Wait! It's not you... I had another hallucination... Lexie!"

She'd gone. Wherever she'd run to hide, he couldn't find her. But in class Elspeth was at her desk, smirking. Todd charged straight over to her, slamming his fists on her desk. Everyone in class jumped. Apart from Elspeth.

"What the hell have you done to me?" he raged. "Tell me, before I…"

Unruffled, Elspeth gazed at him, looking bored. "What? I did what I promised. I got rid of your bad dreams, didn't I? Are you saying you're still having nightmares?"

"No, you witch. Not nightmares. It's real now. I see it everywhere. It's here now, look, hanging from the ceiling."

Webby tried to calm the situation. "Todd, there's nothing there. You're seeing things. It's not her fault. Chill, mate!"

"It *is* her fault! She's some sort of witch."

She smiled. It was a cold, snake-like smile. Cunning and deadly. "Ah! If only I was a witch. I would have such fun. Sadly, I'm only little old me, with one or two powers – special powers."

"I knew it!" Todd gasped, turning to Webby. "Hear that? She's been using powers. It's not me going mad."

Webby shrugged. "I reckon you're both nuts. Leave me out of this."

Todd turned back to Elspeth. "You'd better use those powers to stop me getting these visions, hallucinations – whatever they are. And you'd better stop them right now!"

To his amazement, she didn't argue. "OK, I will," she said simply.

He couldn't believe his ears. "Huh? You will?"

"Sure! Just dump Lexie, go out with me, and all your troubles will be over." She looked him straight in the eye. "So, Todd, what do you say?"

CHAPTER 5

A SIMPLE CHOICE

"What!" Todd exclaimed. "That's blackmail!"

"Call it what you like," Elspeth shrugged. "But that's the deal. Finish with Lexie and go out with me."

"Over my dead body!" Todd gasped.

Her eyes lit up. "If that's how you want it..."

He wanted to lash out, knock her off her chair, stamp on her. "This stops! Understand! This stops right now!"

"OK!" she said, agreeably.

"What?"

"I said OK. I'll make it stop."

"You're not kissing me again!" He knew how stupid that had to sound.

"Spoilsport! But OK, I'll just stroke your forehead. Stroke away all those nasty, frightening visions."

He didn't want her to touch him. But surely she couldn't do him any harm by stroking his forehead, could she? "This had better not be one of your tricks."

He sat down and she stroked his forehead. She didn't sprout talons and rip him to shreds as he'd half expected. But he was glad when she had finished. "There now, you won't ever see that hideous face again, I promise."

He gave her a warning glare. "You'd better not be messing with me."

"I made you a promise, didn't I? You'll never see that awful face again."

Lexie didn't come back into school that day. When he asked the teacher about her, he said she'd gone home, unwell.

Walking home, Todd was terrified to glance up in case the hideous thing was dangling from the telegraph wires like some vile Christmas bauble. He was afraid to open his wardrobe door when he got home. Too anxious to look in the mirror. And when he woke in the night he was terrified it would be lying on the pillow next to him.

But there was nothing there. All gone!

At school next day Webby eyed him warily. "OK, mate? Sleep well?"

"Like a log!"

"No scary faces anywhere?"

"Nope! Not a thing," Todd said cheerfully.

"Good old Elspeth, she stuck to her word this time!"

The other kids were strolling into class. Todd spotted Lexie and his heart plummeted. She looked awful. Exhausted, bleary eyed, nervous. He saw her glance around the classroom. Saw her cringe. Saw her cover her eyes.

He raced over to her. "Lexie!"

She peered out from behind her fingers at him. "It's everywhere," she whispered. "Everywhere I look. In my dreams. In my bedroom. In my bed… Oh Todd! She's cast her spell on me now!"

Todd stared at her, his heart aching. "I'll sort it. Don't worry."

Elspeth wasn't in class yet, and Todd raced out of the room. Running along the corridor, he bumped into her just as she was coming in. He grabbed her, span her round and marched her back outside.

"You win," he uttered. "I can't let Lexie go through all the horror you put me through. So you win."

She looked surprised at first. And then a cold smile spread across her face. "Yes, I thought you'd see it my way. Have you told her yet? Have you told Lexie you're finished with her? Have you told her we're dating now?"

Defeated, he murmured, "I'll tell her now. Only stop her visions. Stop them right this minute. OK?"

"With pleasure." She waved her hand as if she was casting a spell. "I don't have to do that – but it looks good, don't you think?"

He didn't answer. She'd won. Miserably, he dragged himself back into class. Lexie glanced warily at him. He pressed his lips on her hair. "It's over. The nightmares will stop now, Lexie. I'm sorry that had to happen to you."

A look of relief washed over her. Slowly, cautiously she looked all around the classroom. "I think you're right. I can't see that vile head now. What did you say to her?"

He took a deep breath. "I couldn't let you go through that. So I... I gave her what she wanted. Told her we won't see each other any more. I'll go out with her. It's the only way either of us will have any peace..."

The words were scarcely out of his mouth before Lexie was on her feet. "No!" she gasped. "That's blackmail. She can't do that! I'm going to find her!"

She stormed out of the classroom. Todd followed. Elspeth was just strolling along the corridor. Lexie barred her way. "We need to talk."

Ignoring her, Elspeth peered around Lexie to Todd and smiled coyly. "Hi, Todd!"

"Outside!" shouted Lexie, giving Elspeth a push.

With a shrug, Elspeth sauntered back along the corridor, flashing affectionate smiles at Todd every few steps. They headed to a quiet corner near the kitchens. There wasn't another soul about.

"Don't be a sore loser, Lexie," Elspeth said. "You're quite a pretty girl. You'll soon get a new boyfriend."

"You're not having him!" said Lexie firmly. "I don't care if you cast a hundred spells on me. Todd is not going out with you!"

"I think you're about to change your mind," Elspeth said, lunging at Lexie, changing, transforming...

Like in the nightmares, Elspeth's face turned a sickly, greyish-white. Black shadows deepened in her sallow cheeks. Her eyes began to bulge, stretching the tiny veins until they became like a map of red lines. Her mouth widened – too wide – so that a black void opened up like a tunnel into hell. Then teeth – dagger-like teeth – appeared, blood oozing from between them. Thick, dark blood.

Horrified at the transformation, Todd wanted to run, but Lexie recoiled in horror for only a moment. Then she lunged back at Elspeth, her mouth wide like a tiger about to bite a chunk out of its prey. She shrieked into the other girl's face.

Elspeth shrieked back. Lunged again, trying to sink her teeth into Lexie's throat.

Lexie didn't cower away, she fought against the horrific apparition, grabbing Elspeth's hair and twisting her ugly head to the left and the right, as if she was trying to pull her head off her shoulders.

Todd couldn't stand it. They were killing each other. He could feel the pressure building up inside him. And then he erupted. "Stop! Stop this! Stop it! I'm sorry, OK? I'm sorry I humiliated you. I'm sorry I made you cry. I'm so sorry, but stop this. Stop it right now!"

Both girls stopped. Gasping for breath, they both looked at him. Elspeth's ugliness melted away, making her normal again. "Finally!" she sighed, looking at Todd. "Finally you're sorry!"

"Of course I'm sorry. I was sorry the minute I said those things," Todd said, reaching for Lexie's hand. She staggered towards him, exhausted. She clutched his hand and leaned her head on his shoulder.

Elspeth didn't seem bothered. The only important thing seemed to be Todd's apology. "What does it take?" she breathed. "You hurt someone, so you apologise. It's so simple. Why couldn't you see that?"

"I didn't know how to," Todd said, beginning to feel a little ray of hope. Was this really all over? Was an apology all it took to calm Elspeth's rage? "I'm very sorry, Elspeth. I never meant to upset you."

"You remember what you said?" she asked.

"Yes," Todd muttered, feeling so ashamed now.

Elspeth reminded him anyway. "Do you remember saying, *Go out with you! Have you looked in the mirror lately?*"

Lexie cast him a disapproving glance. "Todd how could you? That's awful."

"I know and I'm sorry," he said quietly. "Please forgive me, Elspeth."

She stared at him for a long time. Then, with a small shrug of her shoulders, she said, "OK."

Todd and Lexie exchanged glances, not daring to believe that the nightmares and hallucinations, or whatever they were, had actually ended forever.

Lexie seemed wary. "And you're OK about Todd and me seeing each other?"

Elspeth drew up her shoulders and let them fall. "Ah! So you're seeing each other? How romantic. Well, carry on. Do what you like…"

Todd didn't dare believe his luck. It seemed like the horror was really over. "Well, we'll see you in class then. Glad there's no hard feelings."

Holding Lexie's hand, he headed back towards class. Only then did Elspeth call after him. "Oh! Todd, are you also sorry for that other thing you said to me?"

"What other thing?"

"You know, that you'd have to be blind to date me."

That was the worst bit. He remembered how she'd really crumbled when he'd said that. "Yes, and I'm really sorry for saying that, Elspeth, really sorry."

"That's OK then," she said, smiling. Looking like she was really over it – and over him.

Todd began to walk away again.

"Because it would be awful wouldn't it…?" she called after him.

He and Lexie turned. "What would?" he murmured, feeling cold inside suddenly. Feeling a chill run down his spine.

"Having to be blind to date someone," said Elspeth. "That wouldn't be good, would it?"

"No," he murmured, noticing how dark the sky had become, as if black rain clouds had suddenly rolled in. Lexie's hand tightened around his. She murmured his name.

The darkness seemed to be shrouding Elspeth. Now it was only her eyes that seemed bright. She spoke, "We'd better get into class. Don't want to be late. Be seeing you." And then her eyes narrowed to slits. Like a snake's – only more venomous. Under her breath she added, "But you won't be seeing me!"

THE END